Lost In The Alps

Lost In The Alps

Cosey

ComicsLit

Also by Cosey:
In Search of Shirley:
Vol. 1 $9.95
Vol. 2 $9.95

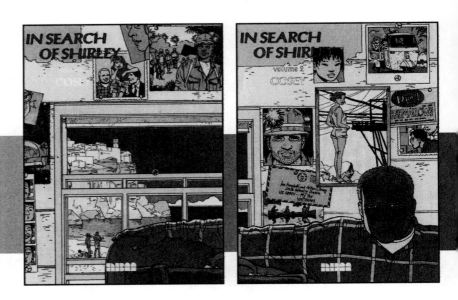

P&H: $2 1st item, $1 each addt'l.
We have over 150 titles, write for our
complete catalog:

NBM
185 Madison Ave. Suite 1504
New York, NY 10016

ISBN 1-56163-160-4
©1984 by PUBLICA-ZOUG
©1996 NBM for the English translation
Translation by Elizabeth Bell
Lettering by Karen Casey-Smith
ORIGINALLY SERIALIZED IN CHEVAL NOIR (DARK HORSE).

3   2   1

Comicslit is an imprint
and trademark of

NANTIER · BEALL · MINOUSTCHINE
Publishing inc.
new york

The Alps of
the Valais,
Switzerland,
just before
1930.

By *cosey*

CHAPTER I

"In time the boys could not even
fly... All the boys are grown up
and done for by this time..."

James M. Barrie

*Fendant: Swiss white wine from the Valais region.

The clock in the church tower was striking seven when Melvin Z. Woodworth reached the village of Ardolaz.

Me and my brilliant wagers!

*Regent: teacher.

That's strange... I'd've sworn somebody was standing over there watching me...

The Grand Hotel had an imposing presence. It was easy to imagine Dragan pacing his room, pencil in hand, swept away by inspiration, composing his Alpine Symphony.

I turned from my daydreams to a guidebook on the Valais Region...

KKKRRRRRR

?

CHAPTER II

"'But who is he, my pet?'

"'He is Peter Pan, you know, mother...
and he is just my size.' She
meant he was her size in both
mind and body; she didn't know
how she knew it, she just knew it."

J.M. Barrie

The fog's getting thicker and thicker. Better go back.

KKKRRRRR

KKRRRRRRRRRRrr

That was a warning!

!

Nature always gives a warning. You just have to listen...

The village is doomed. Got a month more, maybe two. Six, at the most. Don't need an expert t'know that!

I'm not waiting around for them to tell us to evacuate. Ten days from now, I'm gone!

I went back to my room. I didn't even need to open the letter. I could easily guess what it said...

"Dear Melvin,
    Blah blah blah, blah blah... I await with impatience the manuscript of your next novel, which you promised for last spring..."

"...speaking of which, you'll recall the sum I advanced you on your author's fee, and your commitment at that time... blah blah, blah blah blah.
    Your friend and devoted publisher, Virgil G. Ashbury"

Blast him!

Still, I opened the envelope. Apart from a few variations in style, my predictions were right on target.

I gulped down a shot of gin, lit up one of those delicious Havana cigars -- a gift from Virgil G. Ashbury to celebrate the unexpectedly high sales of my first two works -- and tried to think about my third novel.

Hours went by. I lit up a second Havana, but the ideas still wouldn't come...

I opened the window to air out the smoky room, then went back to my armchair. I'd brought a copy of "Peter Pan" with me. I plunged into J.M. Barrie's novel with pleasure. It was a breath of fresh air.

PETER PAN IN KENSINGTON GARDENS ☆ PETER PAN AND WENDY
J.M. BARRIE
DER & STROUGHTON LONDON

Dragan had given me this wonderful book for my tenth birthday, and reading it had a lot to do with my decision to become a writer.

I read till late in the evening, going back to certain passages three and four times.

Midnight already! I'd better stop now, or I won't have any left to read for the rest of my stay.

The snow had been falling for a week.

CHAPTER III

"The fairies are cunning little creatures. They dress exactly like whatever flowers are in season; so that you might look at a crocus, or a hyacinth, or a lily, and never guess that it was really a fairy, because it stood quite still."

J.M. Barrie

Rotten weather!

Some evenings when I hung out in the bistro, sitting at a table until closing time, I wouldn't hear more than a few words spoken.

I jotted down my ideas and a few notes in my notebook.

It was quite an eclectic assortment. I even made an attempt at writing "Page One"... in vain. My attention kept wandering to "Variations on a Serbian Theme," as I'd heard it that night.

A few times, on my walks, I strolled around the Grand Hotel, but heard nothing more.

This night, though, card games and pear brandy had livened up the mood in the small bistro.

North wind tonight... good weather's on the way!

Sure enough, the next day the whole village was at work in the winter sun.

A few days later, I picked out a promising trail and left the village before dawn with a couple of seal skins attached to my skis.

Thin slices of dried meat, some rye bread, cheese with a faintly sour taste, a small flask filled with stream water.

Blue sky, white snow, sun...

Suddenly I felt a clearer vision, an unparalleled lucidity. I was bursting with enthusiasm for life. I wanted to question fate, explore the whys and wherefores of our existence, seek out the common ground of science and spirituality, invent some new art...

I also wanted to become extremely rich and famous.

Once again, I thought of my brother, Dragan. Actually, Dragan was my half-brother, twelve years older than me.

In my mind's eye I saw our tiny apartment in London, a single room, freezing cold... Zoran, our father... His pathetic jobs: chauffeuring one month, gardening the next, making yogurt, and the like. He'd even tried importing caviar with a Russian friend.

Zoran had left Serbia with his son Dragan, determined to make his fortune in the United States. They'd been stopped in London, rejected by American immigration due to a virus. That's where he met the young Englishwoman who later became my mother. Years went by, and his ship never came in.

The aging Zoran placed his hopes in his two sons. Bit by bit, he saved up enough to give us a decent education. Dragan was to become a doctor, myself a lawyer. More than anything, he wanted us to rise above the poverty that was all he'd ever known.

But Dragan had caught another virus: music. He began to compose. One day, he left us to devote himself to his passion. Our father was in despair. Dragan wrote often. He was traveling. Vienna, Salzburg, Paris, Florence, Rome. But we could tell his music brought in barely enough for him to eat.

In the meantime, I devoured every book in the National Library, one by one. I dreamed of becoming a writer. But of course I couldn't mention this to old Zoran.

A few years later, an unusually thick letter arrived. It had been mailed from Sion, Switzerland. Dragan had used the stationery of the Grand Hotel at Ardolaz. His music was now a growing success. He'd put several bank notes in the envelope. Big ones.

From then on, the envelopes came regularly, with the same contents. Good times had arrived. A heated apartment. A fur coat for my mother. We had friends over every night, and--most important-- Zoran gradually forgot about his plans for medicine and the law.

Dragan described his concerts, performed before the most dazzling crowds on the Continent. Our father was exultant. And that's how, thanks to my brother, I was able to achieve my dream.

I studied Shakespeare and Milton at Oxford. I began to write my first essays, using a pseudonym suited to the locale. Vlatko Z. Zmadjevic became Melvin Z. Woodworth.

A year later, Dragan died in an accident as he was taking a bath in the Grand Hotel. A bird's nest had blocked the ventilator of his water heater, and he was asphyxiated by the gas.

I miss you, *Mačak!* *

The glacier was rumbling once a day now...

KKK KRRR

The sun had slowly begun to go down. It was time I did the same.

*Mačak: big cat.

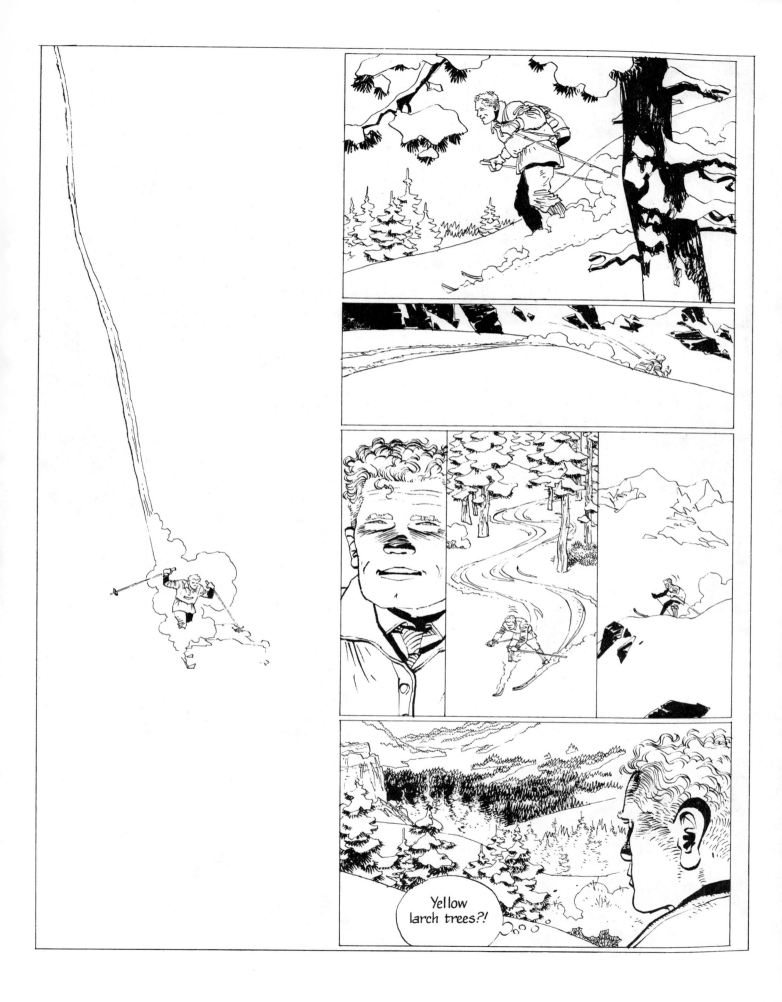

Larches usually lose their needles in autumn. Time seemed to have slowed its pace in this small forest. The air was warmer; the snow gave way to a carpet of moss.

I must have
been dreaming,
but I had
no desire to
wake up.

* *Bisse:* An irrigation canal dug into the earth or built onto a cliff to conduct water to arid fields and prairies during the thawing season.

Pitiful job. Room and board, but not a penny. Hotel guests rollin' in money askin' him to play polkas or whatever's popular... What a waste! Better'n starvin', though.

But what about all that money he sent?

I'm gettin' there. He'd take long walks in th' mountains, all alone. Workin' on his alpine symphony, I guess. We got friendly.

Don't know why, but right around then my old memories started comin' back. Farinet -- dead thirty years, then -- his counterfeit coins, twenty-centime pieces...

Dragan needed money. Me too. I took up th' business again. But I set my sights higher this time: *thunes!* Ha ha!

Yer brother's job was gettin' the coins outta here. He'd go traveling. It was perfect: outside the valley, nobody suspected a thing! Spent the rest of his time on his music.

It was all workin' like a charm. Then one day he gets th' idea of takin' a room at th' Grand Hotel. Thought he'd be a guest for a change...

"The only problem with seeking the truth is that in the end you find it."
I'd put those words into the mouth of the protagonist of my second novel, *Rendezvous in Madrid.*

Remarkable exhibition of skill, Sir Woodworth! But I must admit to a preference for your literary work.

I've been dying to ask you a question, Sir Woodworth: What's the title of your next work going to be?

Huh? Er... *In Search of Peter Pan.*

"In Search of..." Wonderful!! Won-der-ful!! WONDERFUL!!

In Search of Peter Pan... The title came out of my mouth almost involuntarily. But when I thought about it, the words that had slipped out in jest were actually quite meaningful: Dragan had been a sort of Peter Pan figure for me. A kindred soul, at least.

The following day I put on a pair of skis (new ones) for a second adventure...

Needless to say, I wasn't headed just anywhere.

It wasn't hard to find the tracks left by Baptistin, myself, and the two gendarmes.

At last, beyond the huts and their *raccards**...

Aha!!

Now there's a night-bird that seems quite at home on skis...

Hey, I'm even getting good on these myself.

The glacier was roaring more often. You heard it every hour now. Typically Swiss -- a glacier timed like a clock!

KRRAK

Raccard: A raised storehouse on pilings.

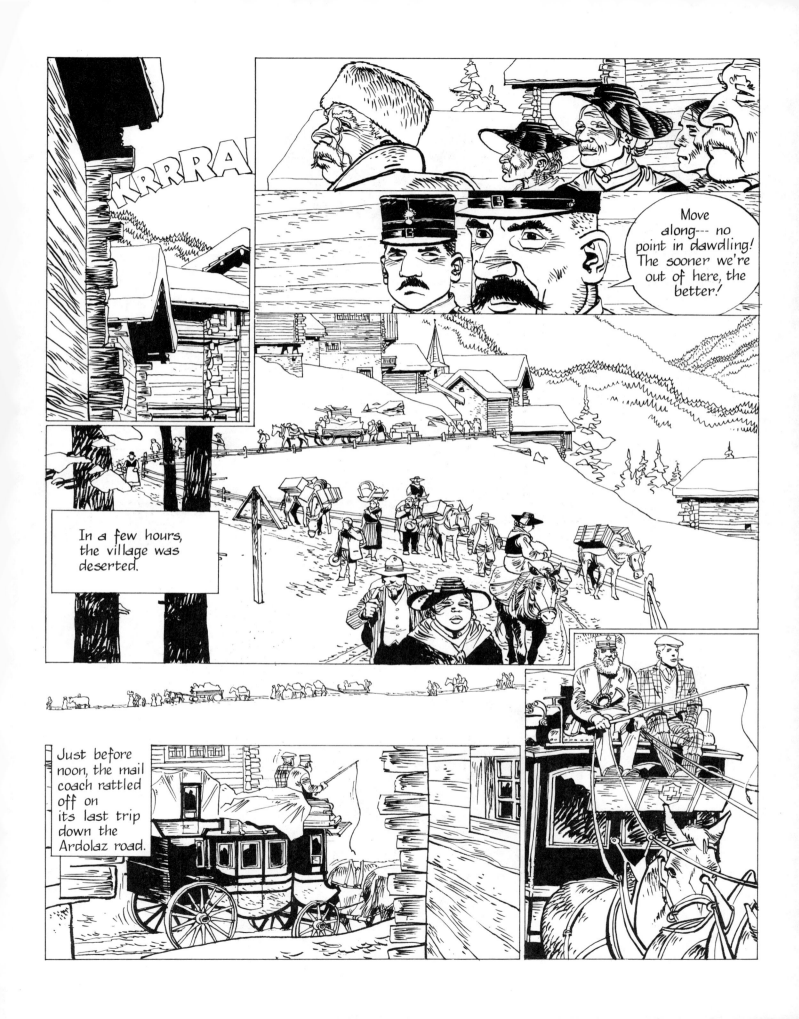

The abandoned valley was sunk in a silence that evoked the end of the world. Only the distant tinkling of a stream could be heard beyond the crunching of my footsteps in the snow.

I'd decided to give myself a few more days. Just enough time to find answers to the questions that this valley seemed to leave hanging over my head.

CHAPTER V

"Listen, then,"
said Wendy....
"There once was
a gentleman--"

"I had rather
he had been a
lady," Curly
said.

"Quiet,"
admonished
Wendy. "There
was a lady
also..."

J.M. Barrie

PENSION DES ALPES

Good old
Zufferey!

I hope it's true that pigs bring good luck. I could use a little!

CHAPTER VI

"Mrs. Darling started up with a cry and saw the boy, and somehow she knew at once that he was Peter Pan."

J.M. Barrie

The owner of the Grand Hotel didn't have bad taste in cigars.

Well, I don't think I forgot anything. All ready... Nothing left but to wait, and hope my hunch is right.

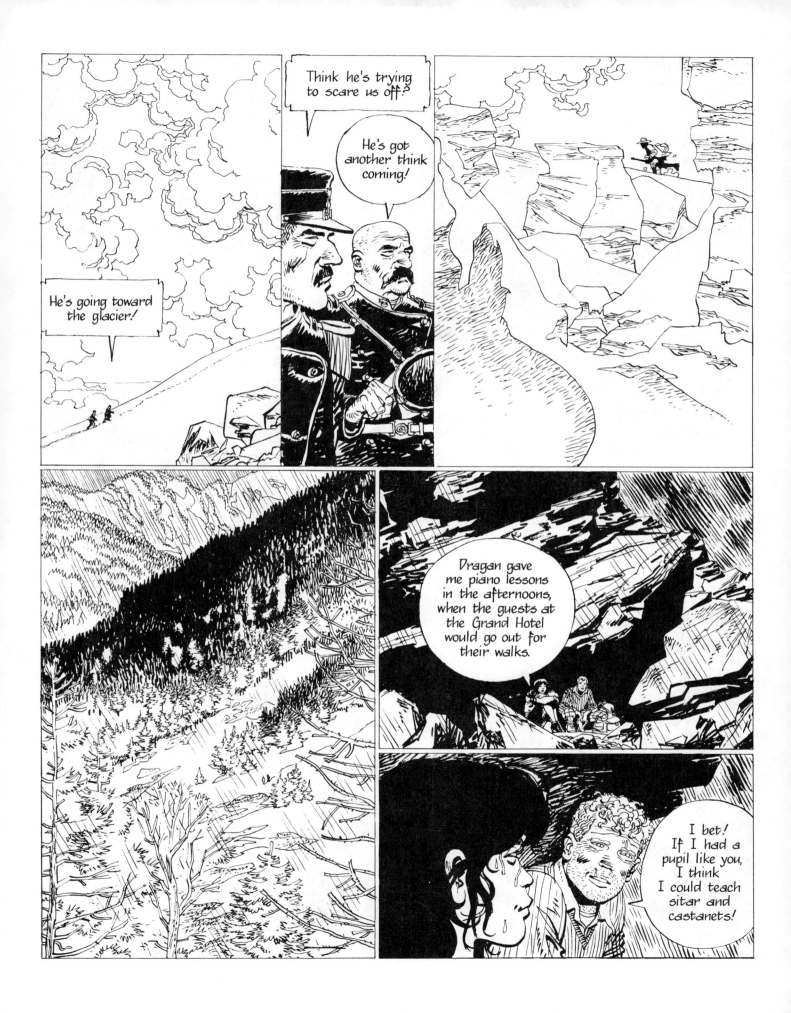

EPILOGUE

"In search of Peter Pan, I found myself astounded and enchanted to have made off with the fairy Tinker Bell in my bags."

Melvin Z. Woodworth

Evolena had prepared herself for the bad news. I shared a great part of her sorrow, and we consoled ourselves with the thought that Baptistin had died happy. From Aoste we went on to Florence.

Evolena was fascinated by everything. She was thrilled by the "Quattrocento," enthralled by Michelangelo. She wanted to visit every museum.

We rented a car and drove by the ocean.

We toured Tuscany, exploring the world of fettuccine, panzarotti, papardelle, pizza, rigatoni, seppia, vongole, scaloppine, calamari, gamberi, gamberetti, prosciutto, osso buco, saltimbocca, Gorgonzola, Parmigiano, Mascarpone, fichi, gelati, granite, and... zuppa inglese.

Evolena laughed at my Oxford accent when I spoke Italian. The young girl from Valais (half-Latin by blood) brightened each day with her laughter and enthusiasm.

The spring sun had transformed my lovely companion. Her beauty was dazzling. She had ideal proportions: the Venus de Milo with arms, no less!

We stayed near the Ponte Vecchio at the Hotel Dante. If that was the inferno, I'd have sold my soul to the devil for eternity.

Pisa...

Rome.

Venice.

I sat down each morning to write in my notebooks. The novel was coming along at a rapid pace. I saw my main character sort of as a precious jewel with countless facets, reflecting a thousand colors from a single light source. Dragan's memory was richly instructive. I thought of Wendy, at night, sewing Peter Pan's shadow.

June. All our money was gone, so I sent my manuscript to Virgil G. Ashbury. His reply was quick in coming, accompanied by a box of Havana cigars and a plane ticket. Ashbury and Studebaker had offered to greet me personally when I arrived at the airport. The apartment on King's Road had been fixed up.

What's more, there was a cottage in Sussex awaiting me. Wilfrid H. Studebaker invited me to choose the wallpaper and, while I was at it, to sign a new contract. The movie rights to my previous novel, *Rendezvous in Madrid*, had been bought by MGM.

August. "The Eighteenth Hole Club." Brighton, Sussex.

I... I feel faint...

Perhaps I shouldn't go horseback riding tomorrow, after all.

I've never felt good about commonplaces, stereotypes, any sort of cliché. But denial of the obvious seemed more odious still. So I had to admit that our tale concluded perfectly in these words: They lived happily ever after, and had many children.

(Peter, Wendy, and Dragan.)

Melvin... What do you think we should choose for a name?

What?! FANTASTIC!! WONDERFUL!!

Cosey
9.1.84

Thanks to François Mattille for his kind contributions to the script.